E Ang
c.1
Angel

P9-CBF-281

The Minotaur of Knossos
/
c1999.

CASS COUNTY PUBLIC LIBRARY
400 E MECHANIC
HARRISONVILLE, MO 64701

A JOURNEY THROUGH TIME

THE MINOTAUR OF KNOSSOS

Published in the United States of America by
Oxford University Press, Inc.
198 Madison Avenue
New York, NY 10016
Oxford is a registered trademark of Oxford University Press, Inc.
ISBN 0-19-521557-5

All rights reserved. No part of this publication may be reproduced, stored in a retrieval system,
or transmitted, in any form or by any means, electronic, mechanical, photocopying, recording or
otherwise, without the prior permission of Oxford University Press.

© 1999 Istituto Geografico De Agostini S.p.A., Novara

English text © 1999 British Museum Press
Published in Great Britain in 1999 by British Museum Press

Published in Italy as *A Spasso Con ... Il Minotauro, Mostro di Cnosso*

Printed in Italy by Officine Grafiche, Novara, 1999

Text and illustrations: Roberta Angeletti

THE MINOTAUR OF KNOSSOS

by Roberta Angeletti

0 0022 0202329 3

Oxford University Press

New York

CASS COUNTY PUBLIC LIBRARY
400 E. MECHANIC
HARRISONVILLE, MO 64701

DR

Hi! My name's Robbie, and my Mom says I'm a super sleepyhead. I'm not really lazy. I just don't like getting up early ... or doing my homework! Today I'm in a good mood, because tomorrow's the start of summer vacation.

Last night I sat down at my desk to do yesterday's history assignment. Homework is such a pain! I had to read about the people of ancient Crete for school. I really wanted to go and play with Pip, my puppy ... But I couldn't. I opened the book and started to read.

To my surprise, I found that the book wasn't boring at all. There
was a great story about King Minos and the Minotaur, a hideous
monster who was like a man with a bull's head. Minos locked the
monster up in a maze to stop him escaping. Everyone who went
into the maze was eaten by him or died trying to find the way out.

Then a hero named Theseus came from Athens to kill the Minotaur. Minos's daughter Ariadne gave Theseus a ball of thread so he could leave a trail and find his way out of the maze ... I closed my eyes, trying to imagine Minos's palace at Knossos.

I must have fallen asleep then, because I suddenly woke up with a loud yawn – and realized that I wasn't in my room anymore! Instead, I was sitting on a big stone seat in a huge hall lined with columns. There was something familiar about the seat ... Yes! It was just like the throne of King Minos that I'd seen in the book!

I looked around. The walls of the hall were covered with paintings of griffins, strange creatures like lions with birds' heads. "Where am I?" I wondered. "And where is Pip?"

"Come on! Doesn't this room mean anything to you?" asked a friendly voice. "And don't worry about your dog. He's just gone to explore."

I looked up in surprise and saw a smiling man in old-fashioned clothes sitting between two pillars. He was drawing and talking at the same time.

"Do you know," he said, "I've been studying the buildings

here at Knossos for more than thirty years now, but I still get things mixed up sometimes. This palace is more complicated than a maze – but if you lend me your pen, I'll draw you a map so you can find your way around." As I listened to him I noticed that he had an English accent.

Now I knew where I was, and I could hardly believe it. I was so
excited – it was fantastic. "I was just reading about this place ..."
I stopped, suddenly realizing who the man was. "But if this is the
palace of Minos, then you must be ..."
The man nodded. "Yes," he replied, "Sir Arthur Evans." And he bowed
politely. "I'm the archaeologist who discovered this place. These days
I spend my time drawing and learning about the Cretan artists.
Look!" And he showed me his drawings of the beautiful wall paintings.

"There you are," Sir Arthur said, handing me the map. "Now you can go and look at the paintings on your own. Oh, and watch out for the Minotaur!"

"Oh, come on!" I sniffed. "Everyone knows that's only an old legend!"

"Well, I'm not so sure," Sir Arthur answered mischievously. "You hear a lot of strange things around here ..."

We said goodbye. With the map in my hand, I wandered off to look for Pip.

But as I went from room to room, I began to feel that I was being watched. I turned around suddenly and spotted a strange boy and girl hiding behind the columns. They reminded me of the people in the wall paintings. Both of them had long, black, curly hair. The boy had a deep tan, but the girl's skin was as white as milk. He was laughing and playing around, but his girlfriend seemed shyer. What were they doing there?

The next room I came to was decorated with beautiful paintings of dolphins and fish swimming in a clear blue sea.
I was just admiring the paintings when I heard voices whispering. It was those two again!
"Look out for the monster! The monster will get you!" they kept repeating. They were trying to frighten me! But why?
I was determined to catch them and make them tell me.

I turned and chased them through the twisting corridors of the palace. But when I got outside they had gone. I stood looking around me. I remembered what I read in my book. This place had once been full of studios and workshops where craftspeople made beautiful things – pots and jewelry, sculptures and paintings. Those things were now in museums all over the world. I forgot all about the boy and the girl as I imagined the luxurious court of King Minos and the feasts and parties he held there ...

"Hello! What are you doing? Playing hide and seek?"
I looked up and saw Sir Arthur watching me from his
seat under a high porch. He beckoned me to go and
join him.

I climbed up to where he was sitting. Looking around, I could
see that a great city had once stood there. Sir Arthur pointed
out the Royal Road, the long street that led from the palace
to the port of Knossos. He described the glittering processions
of kings and foreign ambassadors that had once passed along
it, bringing gifts to the court.

Then he showed me the place where the famous bull-leaping ritual was held. Suddenly he broke off. "Look over there," he said, pointing to a maze of ruins. "That cord ... do you think it could be Ariadne's thread?" He was teasing me again! "More like Pip's leash," I replied crossly.

We scrambled down from the terrace and crept up to the mysterious cord. It WAS a leash! I grabbed it and tugged. "Pip!" I called, "Come on out, you bad dog. It's me, Robbie! I've been looking for you everywhere!"
I pulled and pulled, but nothing happened.

24

Strange! I didn't remember Pip being so strong ...
Sir Arthur took hold of the leash and pulled with me.
"Come along, Pip old chap!" he cried cheerfully. We both
pulled as hard as we could, until suddenly – SNAP! – the
leash broke!

Then ... from around the corner, a huge monster appeared. It had a man's body and a bull's head ... and the look of someone who has just been woken up out of a deep sleep and is angry ... VERY angry! The broken leash was dangling from its neck. "Help!" I yelled, "It's the Minotaur!" In my surprise I fell to the ground, knocking Sir Arthur over and sending his drawings flying around the courtyard. It WAS the Minotaur! And I'd thought it was only a legend!

The next moment, everything had vanished – the palace, the
Minotaur, Sir Arthur, all of it. I looked around and saw that it was
morning, and I was lying on my bedroom floor, with Pip licking me.
Had it all been a dream? I wasn't sure – everything had seemed so
real. When I closed my eyes, I could still see the ruins of Knossos.
When I opened them again, I saw Sir Arthur's map on the floor ...

I didn't get my report done, of course. I tried to explain what
happened but nobody believed me — even when I showed them
the map. But everyone enjoyed my story so much that my
teacher gave me an A for my imagination. She said that when
it comes to telling stories, I'm the best in the class!

WHO WERE THE CRETANS?

THE MAP SHOWS THE ISLAND OF CRETE IN THE AEGEAN SEA, TO THE SOUTHWEST OF GREECE. CRETE WAS THE HOME OF THE MINOAN CIVILIZATION.

Mycenae •

GREECE

Aegean Sea

Knossos

CRETE

THE MINOAN CULTURE OF ANCIENT CRETE WAS ONE OF THE OLDEST CIVILIZATIONS OF THE GREEK WORLD. IT WAS NAMED AFTER THE LEGENDARY KING MINOS, WHOSE PALACE AT KNOSSOS IS THE SCENE OF OUR STORY. THE MINOAN CULTURE LASTED FROM AROUND 3200 BC UNTIL AROUND 1100 BC, ALTHOUGH FROM ABOUT 1450 BC CRETE CAME UNDER THE INFLUENCE OF THE MYCENAEANS ON THE GREEK MAINLAND. FROM ABOUT 1200 BC THE MYCENAEAN (GREEK) PALACES WERE DESTROYED AND THE MINOAN AND MYCENAEAN CULTURES DECLINED.

In Minoan times Crete was home to palaces such as Knossos, Phaistos, Mallia, and Zakros. They were like little kingdoms. Knossos was the most important of the four. The rulers lived in magnificent palaces that were small towns in themselves, with workshops, stores and offices for the scribes and officials who ran the kingdoms. Most of the people lived in the towns that grew up around the palaces, or in country

villages. On the whole, they enjoyed a good standard of living for the time. Minoan women may have enjoyed rights and freedoms that were unknown elsewhere in the ancient world.

The first Cretans were farmers and fishermen, but the island's excellent natural harbors and its position in the Aegean Sea soon made Crete a center of trade and commerce. The Minoans were expert sailors who traveled as far as

Egypt and Syria, the holds of their ships loaded with oil and wine, woollen cloth and pots destined for the courts of ancient Near Eastern rulers. They brought home copper, tin, precious stones, and ivory to be worked by the highly skilled Minoan craftsmen.

The Cretans may have worshipped many deities, including a Mother Goddess. Most of their gods and goddesses were connected with nature: the sun, the moon, the mountains, the caves, the rain, and various animals including the bull, which was a symbol of fertility. One important religious ritual was bull-leaping, a

test of skill in which brave young men took turns to seize a bull by the horns and perform dangerous acrobatic vaults on its body. Some archaeologists believe that this was a magical rite to ward off the earthquakes that often devastated the Aegean islands.

The Palace of Knossos

The palace of Knossos was discovered by the English

archaeologist Sir Arthur Evans – the distinguished gentleman in old-fashioned clothes who appears in our story. The palace was several floors high and covered a huge area. The columns that lined its halls and courtyards were wider at the top than at the bottom, and the walls were decorated with paintings of sea life, plants, flowers, animals, and human figures. The rooms were designed to be cool and shady, offering relief from the hot sun. As well as the king's private chambers there were servants' quarters, offices, barracks for the guards, banqueting halls, workshops and artists' studios, kitchens and storerooms, sanctuaries for worshiping the gods, and even prisons! Some people think that this sprawling tangle of rooms, staircases, and corridors gave rise to the myth of the Labyrinth, the maze where the

Minotaur lived.

Evans' excavations began in 1900. He uncovered not only the palace, but also many other buildings and objects, including hundreds of tablets with ancient inscriptions. During the next thirty years, Sir Arthur devoted himself to reconstructing the ruins and paintings of Knossos. Archaeologists now think that Evans made a number of mistakes in restoring the ruins and paintings – for example, in one painting he thought a blue monkey was a boy!

The Story of Theseus and the Minotaur

According to Greek legend, King Minos was the son of Zeus, the king of the gods. One of the ways the ancient Greeks worshiped their gods was to sacrifice animals to them, and Minos wanted a bull to sacrifice. He prayed to the sea-god Poseidon to send him an animal worthy of the gods. But when his prayer was answered, the bull that appeared was so splendid that nobody wanted to kill it. This upset the gods and made them angry. As a punishment, Zeus made Pasiphae, Minos' wife, give birth to the Minotaur, a monster with a human body and a bull's head. The king and queen hid the Minotaur away inside a complicated maze called the Labyrinth. Everyone who entered the maze was eaten by the Minotaur, or died of hunger while trying to find the way out.

Every nine years, the city of Athens had to send seven young men and

seven young women as a sacrifice to the Minotaur. They were sent into the maze and were never seen again. The hero Theseus was the son of the King of Athens. He was determined to kill the Minotaur and stop this cruel tradition, so he volunteered to join the group of young people sent to Crete. When they arrived, Minos' daughter Ariadne fell in love with Theseus and decided to help him. She gave him a ball of thread so that he could leave a trail and find his way out of the maze. After Theseus killed the Minotaur, he sailed home with the young Athenians, taking Ariadne with him.